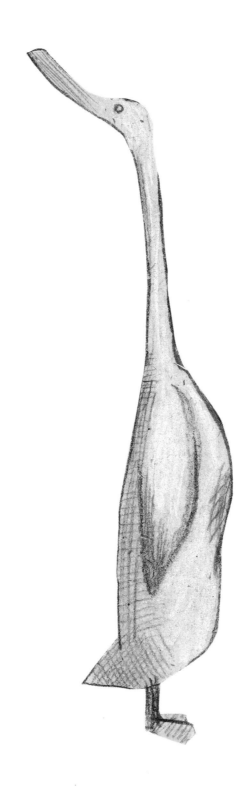

First American edition published in 2011 by Gecko Press USA, an imprint of Gecko Press Ltd.

A catalog record for this book is available from the US Library of Congress.

Distributed in the United States and Canada by
Lerner Publishing Group, Inc.
241 First Avenue North
Minneapolis, MN 55401 USA
www.lernerbooks.com

This translation first published in New Zealand and Australia in 2008 by Gecko Press
PO Box 9335, Marion Square, Wellington 6141, New Zealand
Email: info@geckopress.com

Original title: Ente, Tod und Tulpe
© Verlag Antje Kunstmann GmbH, München 2007
First published in Germany in 2007 by Verlag Antje Kunstmann GmbH. All rights reserved.

Translator: Catherine Chidgey
Editor: Penelope Todd
Typesetting: Archetype, Wellington, New Zealand
Printing: Everbest, China

ISBN hardback (US edition): 978-1-877579-02-8

For more curiously good books, please visit www.geckopress.com

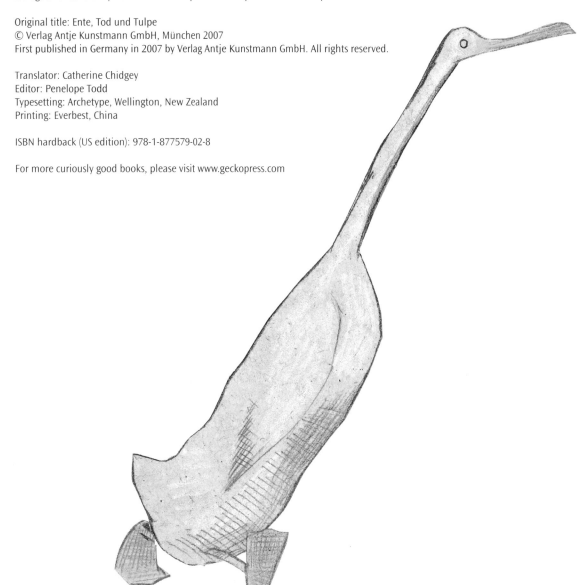

WOLF ERLBRUCH

Duck, Death and the Tulip

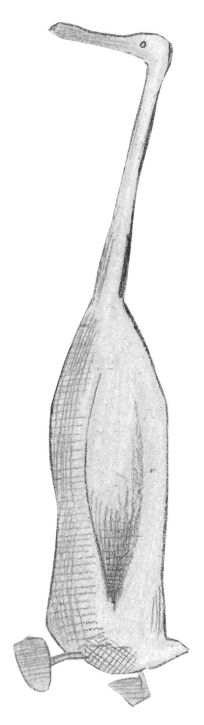

GECKO PRESS

For a while now, Duck had had a feeling.

"Who are you? What are you up to, creeping along behind me

"Good," said Death, "you finally noticed me. I am Death."

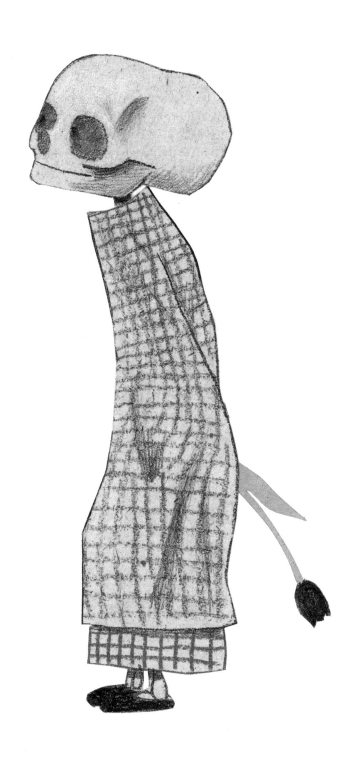

Duck was scared stiff, and who could blame her?

"You've come to fetch me?"

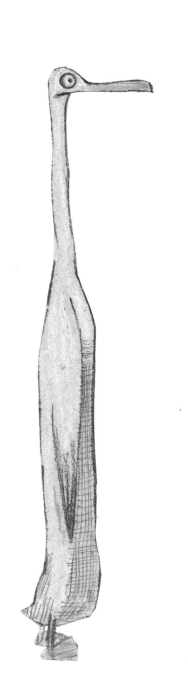
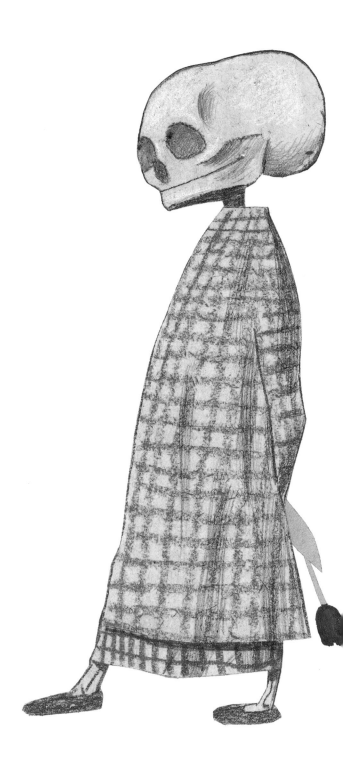

"Oh, I've been close by all your life—just in case."

"In case of what?" asked Duck.

"In case something happens to you. A nasty cold, an accident—
   you never know."

"Are you going to make something happen?"

"Life takes care of that: the coughs and colds and all the other things that happen to you ducks. *Fox*, for example."

Duck tried not to think about that. It gave her goosebumps.

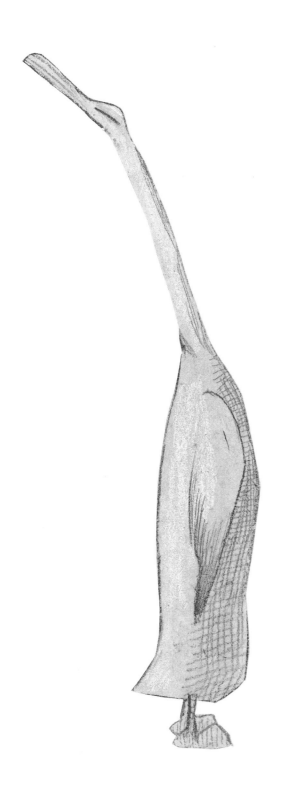

Death gave her a friendly smile.

Actually he was nice (if you forgot for a moment *who* he was). Really quite nice.

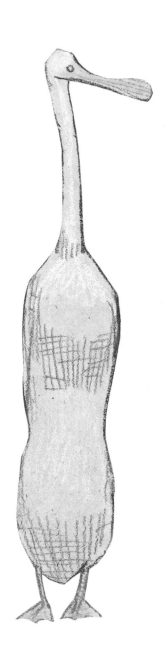

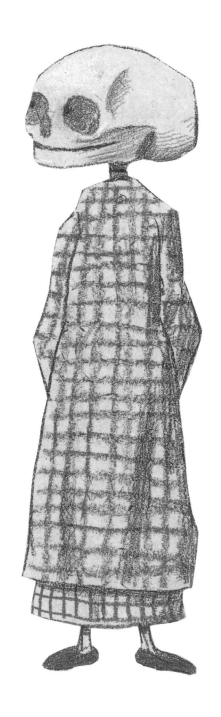

"Shall we go down to the pond?" she asked.

Death had been dreading that.

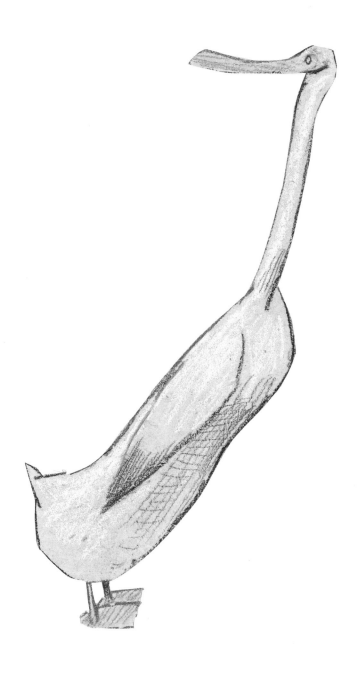

Before long, Death decided that he had his limits.

"Forgive me," he said. "I really must get away from this damp."

"Are you cold?" Duck asked. "Shall I warm you a little?"
Nobody had ever offered to do that for Death.

Duck woke first, very early in the morning.
"I'm not dead," she thought to herself.

She poked Death in the ribs. "I'm not dead!" she quacked, utterly delighted.

"I'm pleased for you," Death said, stretching.

"And if I'd died?"

"Then I wouldn't have been able to sleep in," Death yawned.

That wasn't a nice thing to say, thought Duck.

For a while she refused to speak, but soon she was chattering again.

"Some ducks say you become an angel and sit on a cloud,
  looking over the earth."

"Quite possibly." Death rose to his feet. "You have the wings already."

"Some ducks say that deep in the earth there's a place where
 you'll be roasted if you haven't been good."

"You ducks come up with some amazing stories, but who knows?"

"So you don't know either," Duck snapped.

Death just looked at her.

"What shall we do today?" Death asked.

"Well, let's not go back to the pond. Let's do something really exciting."

Death was relieved. "Shall we climb a tree?" he teased.

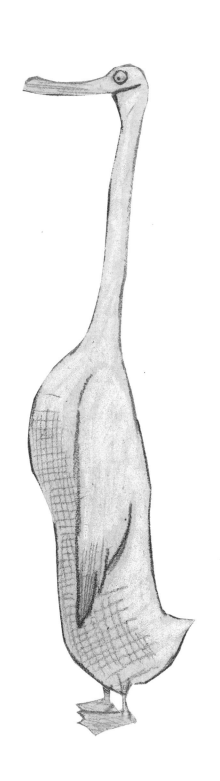

They could see the pond far below.

There it lay. So still. And so lonely.

"That's what it will be like when I'm dead," Duck thought. "The pond alone, without me."

Death could sometimes read minds. "When you're dead, the pond will be gone, too—at least for you."

"Are you sure?" Duck was astonished.

"As sure as sure can be," Death said.

"That's a comfort. I won't have to mourn over it when …"

"… when you're dead." Death finished the sentence. He wasn't coy about the subject.

"Let's climb down," Duck pleaded after a bit. "You can start having strange thoughts in trees."

Summer was ending and they went less and less often to the pond. They sat together in the grass, saying little. When a cool wind ruffled her feathers, Duck felt its chill for the first time.

"I'm cold," she said one evening. "Will you warm me a little?"

Snowflakes drifted down.

Something had happened. Death looked at the duck.

She'd stopped breathing. She lay quite still.

Death stroked a few rumpled feathers back into place,
then he carried her to the great river.

He laid her gently on the water and nudged her on her way.

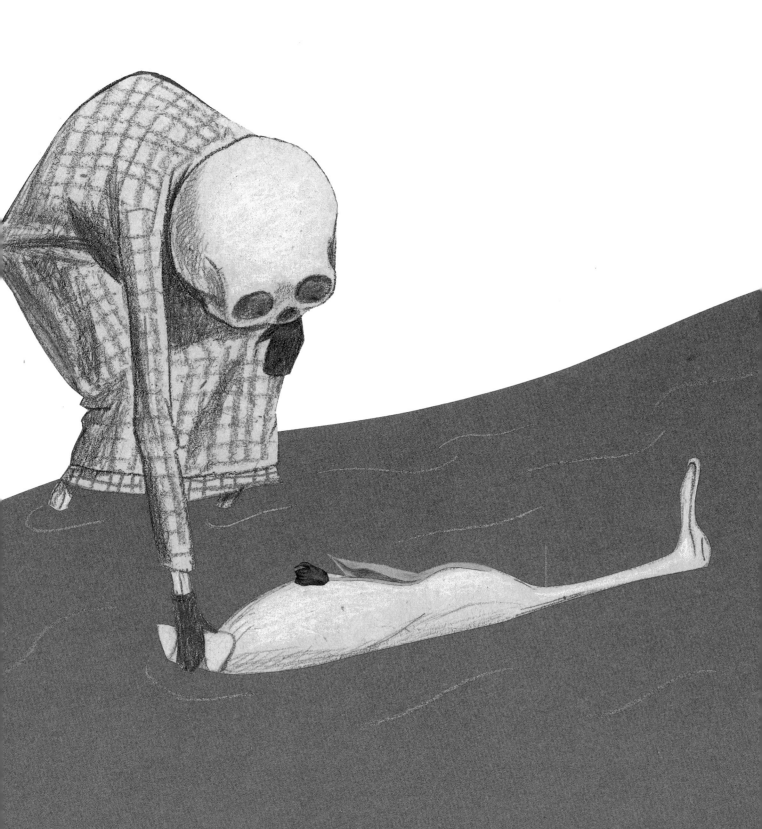

For a long time he watched her.

When she was lost to sight, he was almost a little moved.

"But that's life," thought Death.

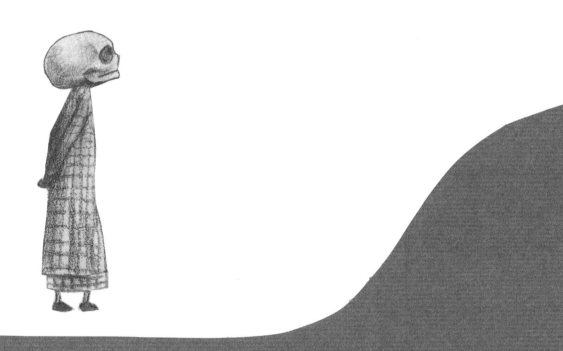